THE SCARIEST MONSTER
IN THE WORLD

Lee Weatherly & Algy Craig Hall

Boxer Books

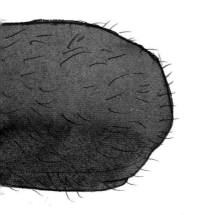

O nce there was a very scary monster.

His fur was wild and weird,
he carried a giant club with bristles on it,
and his teeth were green and mossy because
he never, ever brushed them.

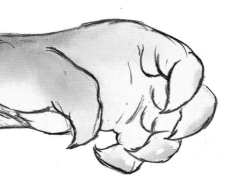

He stomped through the forest and shouted,

"GET OUT OF MY WAY!"

The other animals ran whenever they saw him coming.

"I'm the scariest monster in the world!" said the monster proudly.

But then one day . . .

"HIC!"

Who had made that noise?

It came again.

"HIC!"

And again!

"HIC! HIC! HIC!"

Oh, no! It was HIM!

"HIC!"

"Go away!" shouted the monster.
Everyone always did what he
said when he shouted.

But the hiccups didn't seem to know that.

"HIC!"

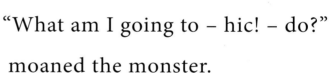

"What am I going to – hic! – do?"
moaned the monster.

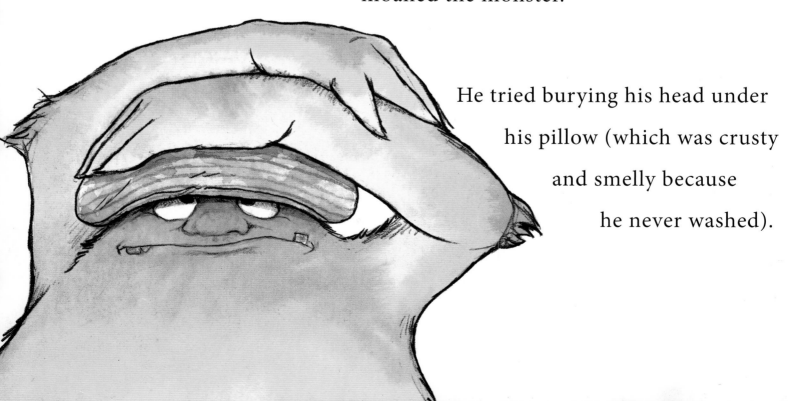

He tried burying his head under
his pillow (which was crusty
and smelly because
he never washed).

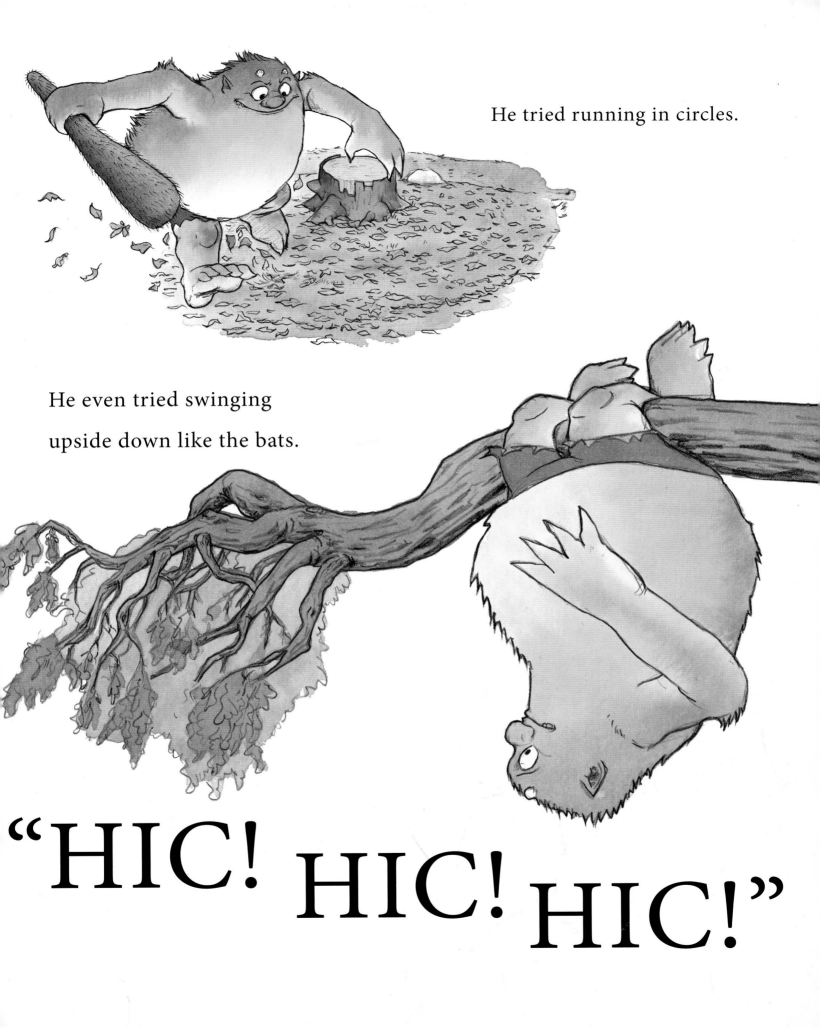

He tried running in circles.

He even tried swinging
upside down like the bats.

"HIC! HIC! HIC!"

Finally the monster sat down and began to cry.

The animals crept out of their hiding places.
"Why is he crying?" they whispered.

"Hic!" groaned the monster. "I've got the hiccups,
and THEY WON'T GO AWAY!"
"But hiccups are easy to cure!" said a clever old crow.

"Really? Tell me how!" begged the monster.

"Just stand on your head and drink a glass of water," said the crow.

But it's hard to drink when you're wrong side up.

"Ack!" spluttered the monster. "I'm – hic! – drowning!"

"That didn't – hic! – work at all," said the monster sadly.

"Try holding your breath!" said the crow.

"Hold it for as long as you can."

WHOOOSH! The monster took a big, deep breath.

"MMMPPP!" he said, flailing his arms.

"Don't give up!" squeaked the mice.

The monster felt dizzy. He staggered in circles.

THUMP!

"He's not hiccuping any more," whispered one of the mice.

The monster sat up and blinked. "They're gone!" he cried.

"The hiccups are . . .

HIC!
AAAGHGH!"

"There's only one thing left," said the crow.

"We'll have to SCARE them out of you!"

The animals tried everything they could think of to scare the monster.

The fox made loud noises behind his back.

The mice made horrible faces and jumped out at him.

The owl told him creepy ghost stories.

"HIC!"

The animals thought and thought. What could be scary
enough to frighten the scariest monster in the world?

"I've got it!" shouted the crow.
"Close your eyes!"

It was very dark
with his eyes closed.

The monster waited and
hiccuped, and hiccuped
and waited.

"This is silly," he thought impatiently.
"They can't scare me."

"Look!" said the crow.

The monster opened his eyes, and . . .

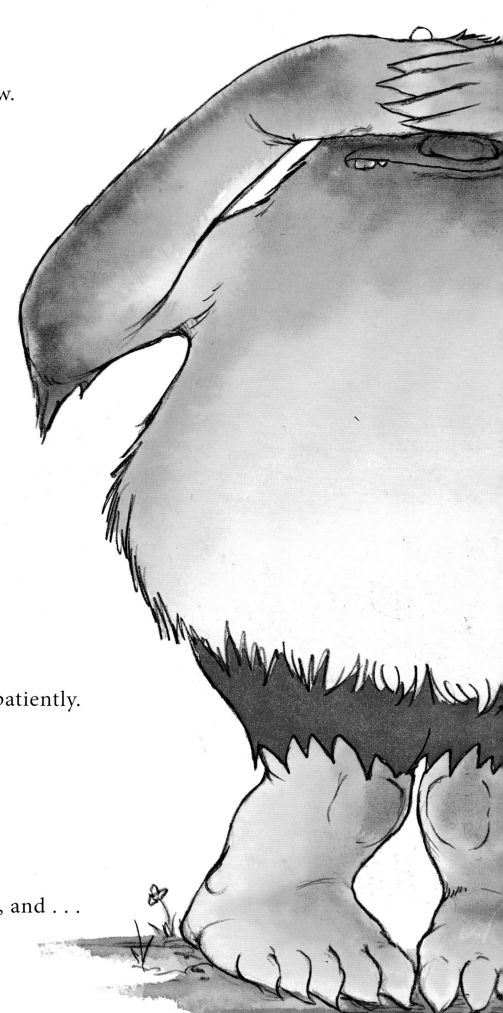

"EEEEK!" he screamed.

Standing before him was a terrible MONSTER.
It had wild, weird fur, and a giant club with bristles
and green, mossy teeth!

"Take it away!" shrieked the monster.

"It's YOU!" laughed the crow.

"You've frightened the hiccups right out of yourself!"

It was true. The hiccups were really gone!

"Hurrah!" sang the monster.

The animals started to slip away.

"Where are you going?" called the monster.

"You're back to normal now," said the crow.

"That means you'll soon be scaring us again!"

The monster thought about how the animals had helped him.

"Don't go," he pleaded. "I don't want to be the scariest monster

in the world any more!"

So he asked the rabbits to help him groom his fur,

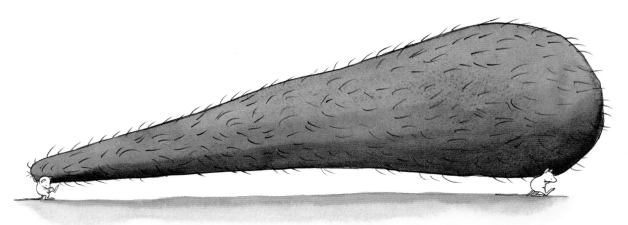

and he gave away his giant club with the bristles on it

and he even brushed his teeth.

Now whenever someone in the forest gets
the hiccups, all they have to do is ask the
monster to come scare them away.
The monster always does, because he can
still look very, VERY scary when he tries.

But everyone knows he's just pretending.